I0556519

A Message of Love

A Message of Love

Uriel Nana

RESOURCE *Publications* · Eugene, Oregon

A MESSAGE OF LOVE

Copyright © 2021 Uriel Mbobda. All rights reserved. Except for brief quotations in critical publications or reviews, no part of this book may be reproduced in any manner without prior written permission from the publisher. Write: Permissions, Wipf and Stock Publishers, 199 W. 8th Ave., Suite 3, Eugene, OR 97401.

Resource Publications
An Imprint of Wipf and Stock Publishers
199 W. 8th Ave., Suite 3
Eugene, OR 97401

www.wipfandstock.com

PAPERBACK ISBN: 978-1-6667-1481-4
HARDCOVER ISBN: 978-1-6667-1482-1
EBOOK ISBN: 978-1-6667-1483-8

09/16/21

Dedicated to all those who sometimes feel like they are not enough. Remember you are loved by the Father.

Though we may feel lost and without compass, God's love encompasses us completely. He loves every one of us, even those who are flawed, rejected, awkward, sorrowful, or broken.

—Dieter F. Uchtdorf

Contents

1

"Teach Me, Lord"

Luke was looking at the auditorium in front of him with mixed emotions. He had been on stage for about five minutes already and no sound had come out of his mouth yet. The congregation had started whispering among themselves about the unusual silence of their pastor. Jide, Luke's assistant, kept trying to make eye contact with him to find out if he needed help of some sort, but Jide's efforts had been in vain. Suddenly, what seemed like a fierce look appeared on Luke's face. His eyes, which had been fixated on the same spot for some time, started moving from one church member to the other. Slowly, the members began to feel uncomfortable: when did their loving pastor turn into a block of ice? The look he was giving each of them from the pulpit was not only cold but disdainful. Finally, he parted his lips and said:

"I am . . ."

He swallowed the remaining words of his sentence and bowed his head.

"Pastor Luke, are you okay?" Jide asked, approaching the pulpit.

"I don't need your help," Luke replied, signaling him with his hand not to approach him.

What on earth had happened to Luke? With his head bowed, he recalled the horrific experience he had had the previous day.

Saturday, March 21, 7 p.m. The leaders' meeting in preparation for the Sunday service had just ended. As usual, Luke had made arrangements for some snacks and drinks to be served to the church leaders in attendance. It was not just a custom for him but a great occasion to fellowship with those he liked referring to as his coworkers. He would enquire of their wellbeing and that of their families and encourage the leaders to share their burdens with one another. As he would always tell them, his goal was to make sure that they were not just involved in church programs but conscious of their identity as Christians wherever they were and whatever they were going through.

"Pastor Luke, I have to excuse myself from today's fellowship. Aban's team is playing today and I'm running late already."

That was Solange, the assistant choir leader. She was a single mom, and her teenage son Aban was part of his school's football team.

"No worries," said Luke with a smile. "Please send my regards to Aban."

"I definitely will, Pastor."

He recalled that he usually gave a ride home to Solange after the meeting.

"How will you get there? Do you want me to ask someone if they are going that way?" Luke asked.

"Oh, don't worry, I will get a cab. Besides, I really have to go now. See you tomorrow!"

Solange rushed out of the room. Luke smiled when he saw how dedicated that young woman was in raising her son. The gathering proceeded in a good ambiance, and after Luke made sure he had spoken with each and every leader present, he dismissed them. He stayed a few minutes after everyone else to make sure everything was in place for the service of the next day, then left.

After getting some food at a restaurant, he headed home. Luke, forty-one years old, had never been married and never intended to tie the knot. Ever since his teenage years, he was convinced that he was neither willing nor called to be married. He knew he wanted to serve the Lord and that the people to whom he would reach out would form his legacy. However, he had once been engaged to a wonderful lady. At that time, he had been serving in a church that needed an assistant pastor for one of their branches. The senior pastor had approached him for the position. He was twenty-three, loved the Lord, and was ready to go wherever he was sent. The only problem was that it wasn't ethically correct for a pastor, whether assistant or lead, to not be married or at least engaged to be married. Their reason was simple: pastoral duties involved counseling to married couples. How would a single pastor handle that?

It was at that point that Luke had asked himself if it was really God's will for him to remain single for the rest of his life or his own desire. "There is nothing bad in getting married and having children," he had thought to himself. "In fact, marriage was instituted by God. Besides, it can help me perform my pastoral duties better." With that, he had approached Laura, a member of the church he was attending. She was a Bible Study leader in the youth ministry, beautiful, caring, and a good friend of his. What more could he look for in a wife? He gave her some time to think about his proposal, and she came back to him a few weeks later to tell him she was willing to venture on the marital journey with him. They announced their engagement in church, and their wedding day was set six months later, so they would have time to go through pre-marital counseling.

Two weeks before their wedding, Laura went to her home town to do some wedding shopping with her mother and perfect the wedding preparations. On her way back three days later, there was a fatal collision between the vehicle in which she was and another whose brakes had failed. Unfortunately, she and all the other passengers did not survive the accident. Although Luke wasn't in love with his fiancée, he cared deeply about her, as one would for a sister. After the funeral, he cut off all his activities and went into a personal retreat. It was there, in a camp located 357 kilometers from civilization, that it was made clear to him as never before. God's love and purpose for him were far beyond his marital status; his decision to marry or not should not have been influenced by ministry ethics or societal norms. How he wished to have understood that earlier! He wouldn't have wasted Laura's time and maybe would have spared her life . . .

Luke sighed when remembering that episode of his life. Had he once regretted his choice of remaining single? Never. Contrary to popular opinion, the life of a single person wasn't filled with boredom and loneliness. As a matter of fact, in his many years of pastoral care, he had counseled several married couples that were feeling lonely and unsatisfied, because they had approached marriage with the incorrect motive of relying on their spouse to be complete. As for Luke, he was fulfilled in his choice of celibacy. Even though it took the church leadership some time to accept his decision to remain single, he was nevertheless given the assistant pastor position a few months after Laura's demise.

Saturday, March 21, 8:30 p.m., Luke's apartment. After eating dinner while watching his favorite comedy show, Luke made a few calls to some of his home friends, as he liked to call them. They were former homeless people who were being cared for by a shelter that Luke was administering. Whenever he had time, he would go visit them in person and pray with them. A number of them were reluctant to come to church, so he didn't mind taking the church to them. When he ended the phone call, he headed to his study to finalize his next day's sermon. Two Sundays ago, he had begun a series on love, and this was the final leg of the preaching. As usual, he prayed for the message to reach out to people in the way they needed it most.

While going through his notes, he started feeling uncomfortable. He first thought he had a stomach upset caused by the food he had eaten. But he realized his uneasiness wasn't physical. It was about his message.

"Do you know Love?" he heard.

He turned and saw no one. The voice was still, yet assertive. Melodious, yet firm.

"I do," replied Luke, thinking he was talking to himself.

"Do you know Love?" The voice was louder.

"I do!" Luke said louder, to match the voice's volume.

"Luke. Do you know Love?"

At that point, the consciousness of the presence of God overwhelmed Luke. He didn't know how nor when, but he found himself on his knees.

"Teach me, Lord," he murmured.

There was utter silence. He could not tell how long it lasted. All he knew was that his eyes were closed. He had expected the Holy Spirit to take him through the Scriptures and explain them to him from an angle he had never understood them before. He didn't know he had rather signed up for a surreal experience. When he opened his eyes, he was not in his study anymore . . .

Luke couldn't recognize the place at first. Apparently, he was in a dining room, and people had just finished eating. He heard laughter from the living room and recognized the person's voice. Solange, the assistant choir leader, was sitting on her couch and talking joyfully over the phone.

"Hi, Solange!" He said, all smiles. "I know it sounds unbelievable, but I don't know how I found myself here."

She kept talking on the phone and paid no attention to him whatsoever. In fact, it was like she didn't know there was someone else in her living room.

"Am I dead? Or is this a vision? But why does it seem so real?" All sorts of questions were going through Luke's mind.

"Listen and watch," said the same voice.

Luke heard a door opening and someone whistling while walking in the direction of the living room. "That must be her son Aban," Luke thought.

To his greatest shock, he discovered that his assistant Jide was the one. What was he doing in Solange's house at this time of the evening?

2

Pretences and Pretexts

"I LOVE YOU, HONEY, bye!" said Solange before hanging up.

Jide came to her all smiles and kissed her.

"Jide! Aren't you married to Elise!?" Luke shouted.

But neither of them could hear him.

"It was a good thing that you sent Aban to your mum for the weekend," said Jide, putting his arms around Solange's waist.

"Yeah, I was tired of going to the hotel. I figured my house would be better," replied Solange.

"After nine months together, we deserve to have some space of our own," Jide said, as he continued to kiss his lover.

Luke recalled that Elise and Jide had been married for a little more than a year. Solange was Elise's good friend and had served as her maid of honor. If he heard rightly, their affair had started just a few months after Jide's wedding. Luke couldn't believe his eyes and ears. Jide, his five-year long assistant, had been lying and cheating. How about Solange? The single mom who sang in the choir, who taught the youth and teenagers on sexual purity, was having an affair with a married man, her friend's husband, for that matter. How could that be?

"Nine months?" said Solange, laughing. "So, the night before your wedding doesn't count?"

"What?" thought Luke. "Then why did he even get married to Elise?"

———

In the space of a nanosecond, Luke was taken back to two years ago, with the surreal impression of watching a movie in front of the biggest screen he had ever seen.

To be more precise, it was around the time when Jide and Elise had started dating. Elise Wells, twenty-seven years old, was the only child of a wealthy couple. When her parents had passed in her teenage years, she had inherited a mighty fortune. If money was not a problem for the frail and beautiful lady, it was however not of help to her personal life. With no siblings or close family relations, she had often fallen into the hands of bad friends who were only around her for her parents' money. But Jide was different—or so she thought . . .

Elise had met Jide at the period of her life when she had decided to cut ties with the pretentious lifestyle to which she had been accustomed. She had taken up a regular job in the marketing department of one of her parents' companies and had even decided to engage in normal activities she had never done before. Thus, on a Friday evening after work, she stopped at a bowling center with the intent to watch how it was played. After about twenty minutes of observing different teams playing against each other, she heard someone coming towards her and asking, "Would you like to play?"

When Elise lifted her eyes to see who the person was, she felt like her heart skipped a beat. Standing in front of her was a tall and good-looking young man wearing a blue and red uniform.

"N . . . No, thanks, I don't know how to play . . ." She managed to answer.

The man gave her a smile, revealing the cutest dimple Elise had ever seen.

"If you're willing to play, I can teach you," he offered.

She nodded in the affirmative.

"My name is Jide, I am one of the bowling coaches. The first one-hour session is free. If you decide to stay with us subsequently, you can go through the registration process at the counter."

Elise nodded to show her approbation. He gave her a pair of bowling shoes and taught her the basics of the discipline. The session was so agreeable that Elise felt the hour passing like five minutes.

"You're really a fast learner," Jide complimented her at the end of the session. "I hope you will stay with us for the next sessions."

"Definitely!" Elise acquiesced.

Without a doubt, Elise registered at the bowling center and chose Jide as her personal instructor. They were having two sessions a week, and both of them were always looking forward to their next encounter. It took Jide about three weeks to ask Elise on a date, which, of course, she accepted. For their first date, they had dinner at a nice restaurant, then went for a walk to a park that was just a few steps away from where they had eaten. They spent at least three hours getting to know each other in a pleasant atmosphere. That night, on the way back to their respective homes, it was obvious to both of them that they wanted to see each other more often.

Jide was funny, down-to-earth, and charming. From the first date, he let her know he was a Christian and shared with her the values in which he believed. After a few weeks of them seeing regularly, Elise told him about her parents' demise and the fact that she had inherited the majority shares in the companies her parents owned.

"I knew you weren't just a marketing intern!" was all Jide answered her, laughing.

Even after she made that revelation, Elise's financial status did not seem to matter to Jide. He had not even once tried to take advantage of her wallet. Whenever they went out, he would foot the bill without thinking twice. If she suggested to pay even half, he would gently remind her that it was his responsibility. Besides, he knew how to listen to her, show her respect, and give her all the attention she needed.

Approximately three months after their relationship started, Jide invited her to the church he was attending and introduced her to the main pastor, Luke, whom he was assisting. Elise felt at ease and gradually got involved in the church community. She even found a good friend in Solange, an amiable single mother who was just two years older than she. After eight months of courtship, Jide proposed to Elise on her birthday, and Solange was the first to be informed. Little did the young woman know how jealous Solange was of their relationship. Solange had set in her heart to seduce Jide and make him hers.

"She can't have the good looks, the money, and the nice guy all for herself!" Solange thought.

Bewildered, Luke watched on the screen how her plan was initiated on a Saturday evening after the leaders' meeting. With the pretext that Luke was having a counseling session, she asked Jide if he could give her a ride home. While in Jide's car, Solange feigned receiving a text message and began sobbing silently.

"Any problem?" asked Jide, concerned.

"No . . . Yes . . . I mean, it's just Aban's father!"

She began crying uncontrollably when she tried to explain how she had been physically and emotionally abused by her ex-boyfriend, who happened to be her high school sweetheart. She had left the five-year long relationship to save her life and that of their son, Aban. According to her, however, he still was not letting them be after all these years. Jide spent hours listening to her and comforting her before going home. From that day, Solange began looking for excuses to get Jide to spend as much time as possible with her son and her, under the guise that Aban needed a male figure to look up to.

As his wedding date approached, what Jide thought to be just empathy for Solange turned out to be romantic feelings. Not only was Solange more mature than his fiancée, but he also felt so useful when he was around the single mom and her son. With his ego being flattered and his increasing proximity to the mother and son pair, Jide rapidly became conflicted. However, one thing was clear to him: he knew that he couldn't renounce Elise. She was the heiress of hundreds of millions. Who would be stupid enough to let go of her? Even though he acted totally uninterested, Jide had already envisaged his luxurious lifestyle after his wedding with Elise. Now that he had fallen for Solange, he had planned to get the best of both worlds. He would marry Elise, entertain her illusions for a few months after their wedding, then divorce her and take half of her properties, as they had decided not to sign a prenuptial agreement. Meanwhile, he could still be with Solange secretly until his divorce was pronounced. All he had to do was to play the good husband for as long as possible, and when the time would come, he would frame Elise to make everyone believe that she was the cause of their marriage not working.

After seeing all that, Luke recalled that Jide had been complaining lately of Elise being a "thorn in his flesh." During some of the post-wedding counseling sessions Luke had had with Jide, Jide had told Luke that he did not feel respected by Elise and was not sure he had made the right choice. So, was that all part of his plan?

In shock, Luke watched Solange and Jide sitting on the couch in Solange's living room.

"Of course, it does count," answered Jide, laughing flirtatiously at his mistress.

"So, when are you divorcing that fool you call a wife?" asked Solange with a provocative voice.

"Soon, my love. For now, let's get into some other business!"

Solange chuckled, and her lover carried her to the bedroom.

All of a sudden, the surroundings changed and Luke found himself back in his study.

"Was that . . . real?" He thought, troubled.

Still in shock, he touched the study table and the objects surrounding him, wondering if he could feel them. He looked around him. Nothing seemed to have changed. He suddenly felt that the scene he had witnessed was unrealistic. He must have imagined it.

"I should stop watching that comedy show," he told himself. "It may be affecting my sanity."

Just when he was about to rule this episode out of his mind, his phone rang. It was Elise, Jide's wife.

"Hello, Pastor Luke. I'm so glad you picked your phone," said Elise, with a troubled tone.

"Hi, Elise, how are you doing?"

"Not so good. I've been calling Jide but he's not answering. I thought that since you're with him, you could tell him to pick his call or give him the phone . . ."

"With him?" Luke said, frowning.

"Yes, for your usual Saturday evening prayer meeting . . ."

Luke exhaled heavily. He had not imagined the scene he had just witnessed. Jide was actually cheating on his wife and was using a supposed meeting with him as alibi.

"I don't know why your meeting took so long today, but I need him to stop by the pharmacy . . ." Elise continued.

Luke was so dumbfounded that he did not hear the rest of the sentence. All he managed to say was:

"Sorry. G . . . Good night, Elise."

He ended the call and sat down, still trying to process everything.

"Luke, do you know Love?" he heard again.

"What do you mean!" Luke asked, upset. "What has Love got to do with two members of my church lying, cheating, plotting, being hypocrites, pretending to be what they are not!"

Luke was a meek person. He almost never lost his temper, and it was difficult to get him upset. But everything he had seen and heard in the past few minutes was getting too much for him to take in.

"Why did you show me all that now, Lord?" he said, sighing powerlessly.

"Watch and listen."

3

The Perfect Match

IN LESS THAN A second, Luke found himself in what looked like a ballroom. People were dressed elegantly, and all looked like upper-class citizens. Luke looked around to see if he knew anybody, but all he saw was a sign posted at the entrance that read, "Welcome to the LYNNS' Charity Gala."

Luke smiled. Stephanie and Roger Lynn, along with their two daughters, were the perfect model of a Christian family. The couple had been married for twenty-four years and yet seemed like high school lovers. Roger was a successful businessman and Stephanie a well-known author and conference speaker. They both attended the church Luke was pastoring and were resourceful in a number of ways. Apart from regularly making donations for the running of the church and the wellbeing of its most indigent members, they often organized couples' seminars and retreats where they would share their experience on how to build and sustain a successful Christian home, not to talk of charity events like these, which they spent months to prepare, only to give all the proceeds to orphanages and shelters. Their eldest daughter Emily was in her third year in a prestigious college, and the youngest Zoe was in her final year in high school. They were both multi-talented, and when they were around, they were always actively involved in the youth group of the church. Needless to say, many people looked up to the Lynn family in numerous ways. Luke thought, perhaps God had brought him there to enhance his message on Love by witnessing the Lynn's family life. He was far from imagining what awaited him.

In what seemed to be like five seconds, the charity gala ended, and Luke found himself in the Lynn's limousine with the couple. Needless to say, that they could neither see nor hear him.

"If we remove all the expenses incurred, the total we got is $15,757,000," Stephanie said, happily.

"Good. Announce on our social media pages that the total of $8,757,000 will be given to the associations we selected before the gala," ordered Roger.

"Roger, you can't keep seven million for yourself again!" protested Stephanie.

"Myself? The house you live in, you and your daughters' high tastes, how do you think I pay for it?" Roger said, enraged.

He continued: "When your stupid daughter committed abortion and developed complications, who spent money to fly her overseas for treatment?"

"You can't say that, Roger. Zoe is your daughter too. And we needed to protect the family's image . . ."

"My daughter!" said Roger, scoffing. "God knows where you got that bastard from!"

Stephanie did not say a word in reply and took out her phone to make a post about the just-concluded event on social media platforms.

"What? Are you missing your lover already?" said Roger, mockingly.

"Roger, stop that please!" pleaded his wife.

"You think I didn't see you flirting throughout the gala? Everybody saw you drinking alcohol and laughing like a fool at Senator Mike's dry jokes!" Roger shouted.

"For the love of God, Roger, I . . ."

He didn't give her time to finish her sentence and forcefully grabbed her hair with his right hand, coercing her to look straight into his eyes. He pressed his left hand on her neck, making it difficult for her to breathe.

"How many times did I tell you that you can do whatever you like in private but must protect our image in public?!" he yelled.

Luke was taken aback by the swiftness and the ruthlessness of Roger's action. The man had always behaved as though he couldn't harm a fly. Seeing the frightened look in Stephanie's eyes right in front of him made Luke wonder how often her husband was brutalizing her.

"We must appear happily married and successful at all times," answered Stephanie, gasping for breath.

Luke watched the scene in disbelief. Stephanie's mechanical response had made her look like an actress rehearsing her script. But, wait. Wasn't that just as it seemed?

Indeed, the Lynn family was exactly how they appeared: too good to be true! They were giving people what they wanted to see and hear in exchange for fame and admiration. They had been putting on a show for so long that they couldn't even remember when it all started. As Stephanie struggled to release herself from her husband's grip, she recalled how she had been the trigger of this whole masquerade.

Luke was once again taken to the past through the surreal screen. He saw how a little over ten years back, the Lewins were nothing more than a normal family of whom no one had heard. At that time, Roger Lewin had been a civil engineer for twelve years, loyally working for the same company all those years, until he was fired. The only reason he was given was that the company needed to downsize. His wife Margaret was an English teacher in a public high school, a job which gave her time to take care of their two daughters.

After losing his job, Roger used his savings and a bank loan to establish his own building company. For two years, he made no profit, and the entire family depended on Margaret's income. As she had to take a second job to support her family, Margaret became stressed, depressed, and addicted to alcohol. It didn't take long for her to suffer from an intoxication and be admitted into a rehabilitation center. Fortunately, around that time, Roger's company launched its first big construction contract, and things came back to the way they were before he had lost his job—or almost.

When Margaret's time in rehab was over, her husband formally prohibited her from resuming work. To him, she had made enough sacrifices for the last two years, and now that he was able to provide for his family, she had to take some rest and solely take care of their daughters. She came back home revived, only to substitute her addiction to alcohol with another type of addiction.

With the services of his company becoming more in demand, Roger was often away from home. If Margaret was happy in the beginning to have more time for herself, she quickly realized it wasn't so fun to stay home all day long and do a lot less than what she had been used to. As she had always loved writing but had not really had time for that in the previous years, she reconnected with that old passion of hers. While looking for ways to publish and market her works, she found out that building a social media presence had become essential to market any kind of product, and she registered on different platforms. "Margaret Lewin is not stylish enough," she thought. She opted to use her middle name, Stephanie, and a classier version of her husband's name, Lynn. She dyed her hair blonde, lost some pounds, and started wearing contacts in lieu of her classic teacher's pair of glasses.

Margaret Lewin was a stay-at-home wife struggling to find a meaning to life. Stephanie Lynn was a philanthropist, an author, a life coach, the wife of a godly and wealthy entrepreneur and mom of two talented and brilliant girls. Not a day would pass without her sharing pictures and videos of her family, each of them more creative or good-looking than the previous. What started as a hobby quickly turned into an obsession. She was always looking for the next interesting thing to entertain her virtual friends and followers. And the least that could be said was that people loved it.

The family quickly started reaping the benefits. When Stephanie announced the launch of her book, she had more than five thousand pre-orders in less than a week. Her husband's business had gained more exposure and was getting more deals than ever. Her daughters were the cool kids all their friends wanted to hang out with. All thanks to the Lynns' fairy tale. But they did not intend to stop there. They needed to create more illusions about themselves. Illusions that would match up and even exceed the ever-increasing expectations of their audience. Illusions so real that no one would be able to dissociate what was true from what wasn't, not even themselves. In fact, all they wanted, was to be loved for who they were not.

Of course, they now needed to buy the house and rides that suited their style, partner with charity organizations to make their philanthropist claim more credible, register their daughters for countless activities, whether they were interested in them or not. With everything getting bigger and looking better and happier, everyone started asking them questions about the key to their picture-perfect life. One day, as she was going through the comments section on one of her posts, Margaret was stunned.

"Have you seen that?" asked Margaret to her husband, showing him her smartphone.

The forty-five-second video extract of their last family date night had attracted 500,000 views in less than two hours.

"Look at all these compliments in the comments sections," noticed Roger with amazement, scrolling through.

"So many of them are asking relationship-related questions," continued Margaret.

"Well, it's time we gave them some answers."

The couple saw an opportunity in that public request and found their new product: happiness! They made up recipes and shared embellished versions of their family's experiences in order to sell their secret to the world through articles and live conferences.

But the truth was, the more beautiful it looked on the outside, the uglier it was on the inside. Roger and Margaret had not been romantically interested in each other for a long while now, and weren't applying any of the formulas they were serving their audience to rekindle the flame between them. In private, Roger was treating Margaret more like a business partner than anything else. Whenever he felt she wasn't representing their so-well-built image, he would either rain abuses on her or hit her. But to Margaret, the fame and prestige that resulted from their pretence had to come with a price she was ready to pay.

Their daughters, who were the only witnesses of the couple's hypocrisy, were bribed by the latter to shut their mouths on any dysfunctionality in the family. But being just teenagers, they were not as comfortable as their parents to play roles. So Emily had chosen to go to a university on the other side of the country, to be the farthest possible from that life of deceits. Zoe, on the other hand, had found refuge in the wrong company and had gotten herself into trouble many times. But no one had ever heard of her wrong-doings, as her parents were always clearing their family's name by all means. Roger intended to use their popularity to run for mayor in the upcoming elections. Therefore, he had to protect his family's image at any cost.

Luke saw Stephanie silently wiping the tears that had dropped down her cheek.

"This is the life of lies I signed up for . . ." she thought, shaking her head.

As he was still trying to wrap his head around what he had just seen, Luke found himself elsewhere.

4

The Dream Life

IN THE TWINKLING OF an eye, everything around Luke changed again. He realized he was at a shopping center. When he turned around, he recognized a younger friend of his, Samantha. She was shopping in a luxurious boutique. He saw the shop attendant giving special attention to Samantha, as though she was some celebrity.

"This is the latest item of the collection. It came out just a few hours ago. I'd sell my arm to get this!" said the attendant, jokingly.

"Luckily for me, I don't have to sell my arm to get it," Samantha replied proudly, "I'll take it."

The attendant broke out in a large smile, just thinking about her commission for the sale she was about to make. She took Samantha's card and processed the payment.

Luke, who had observed the scene, recalled that Samantha had started working for a finance firm as a junior accountant just a few months ago. Knowing her relatively modest financial situation, he knew she could not afford the bag she had just purchased. From where was the money coming?

Just like it had happened at Solange's place, Luke began seeing scenes of Samantha's life.

He saw on the big screen the first time he met Samantha. He had been on his way to his office that day and had stopped by a café to grab something to eat. While waiting for his order, he saw a young lady sitting at a remote corner with her head bowed. He observed her for a few seconds before realizing she was crying soundlessly. After receiving his order, he walked silently towards her and stood across from her.

"May I?" he asked, pointing to the chair opposite hers.

She nodded her head without lifting it up. He sat there for thirty minutes without saying a word. Unknown to the young lady, Luke was praying for her in his heart. When she finally lifted her head, she was surprised to see that he was still sitting there.

"Do you want a hot cup of coffee?" he asked her, not minding her questioning look.

She shook her head in the negative and turned to her bag, ready to gather her belongings to leave.

"I know a place where you can live without paying anything," he said calmly.

"What! How do you . . . ?"

All he did was exhibit a warm and friendly smile in return. The truth was, while the young lady had her head bowed, he had noticed that her bag was open, and a paper on which was written FINAL EVICTION NOTICE could be clearly seen. He quickly figured out that she had been thrown out of her apartment.

"My name is Luke, and I'm here to help," he said, still with a calm and reassuring tone.

Besides his harmless appearance, there was something more about Luke that made Samantha feel comfortable with him, despite just having met him. And in less than no time, Luke became not just her benefactor but also something close to the father figure she had never had. Indeed, Samantha's mom didn't believe in love and relationships, but desired children. She had therefore gone to a sperm bank and a doctor and had gotten herself inseminated. Not just once, but on three different occasions. So, Samantha grew up with no father and a mother who believed she was all her kids needed in life.

Aside from the eighteen-year difference that existed between them, Luke had indeed treated her like his own daughter. Samantha often wondered why a man with such a big heart had not built a family of his own. The day they met at the coffee shop, he took her to the shelter he was administering and made sure all her immediate needs were covered before leaving her to rest. Throughout the weeks she spent there, he would either visit her personally or call her to make sure she lacked nothing. Their conversations were always filled with warmth and laughter. He was ever ready to listen to her without judging her. Through the Bible studies that were held regularly at the shelter (the Love Home, as Luke liked to call it), Samantha learned so much about God and his love for her and how to respond to it. She joined the church that Luke was pastoring and became a volunteer. Having studied accounting in college, she started by assisting Martina at the church treasury. When Martina moved to another town with her family, Samantha was put in charge.

After taking a couple of menial jobs, she ended up getting one in her field. The salary wasn't too great, but at least she was able to leave the shelter and get an apartment of her own. How excited she was when she got the confirmation letter from that finance firm! Little did she know where it would land her.

Another scene unfolded before Luke's eyes. Sitting on an office chair, Samantha was carefully reading a document from a desktop computer when a lady came right beside her office space.

"Are you going out for lunch?" asked the young woman named Claire.

Samantha had been working at the Deer & Partners finance firm for six weeks, and she had never gone out for lunch. Meals in restaurants around their office were pricey, and the young woman had so much to care for with her modest salary that she couldn't afford them. Thus, she was bringing a homemade sandwich every day and eating it at her desk at break.

"No, thanks," answered Samantha, with a forced smile.

"Oh, I forgot you can't afford a meal!" said Claire, with her voice loud enough to be heard by the majority of the workers of the firm.

After emitting a mocking laugh, she turned stylishly, grabbed her expensive bag, and left for lunch, leaving Samantha red with shame and anger. Claire Deer never missed an opportunity to make humiliating remarks to remind Samantha of her financial status, and there was nothing the young lady could do about that. The pretentious Miss Deer was the daughter of the firm's principal partner. Undoubtedly, she was using her dad's money to purchase all the overpriced items she liked to show off.

Even though Samantha was proud of making a decent living by herself, she couldn't help but feel downgraded by Claire's incessant comments. To make things worse, she received a video call from her mother Bertha that day on her way back home.

"I thought by now you'd have your own car," her mom said with a disdainful expression, when she noticed Samantha was using public transportation.

"Hi, mom," Samantha replied, embarrassed.

"And what was the point of moving to a big city if you can't even wear good-looking clothes," Bertha continued.

"How are you doing?" asked the young woman, ignoring her mother's comment.

"I'd be better if I didn't have to worry about your siblings and you. Samantha, I sent you to one of the best schools. I'd expected you to have a good job and support your younger siblings, but here you are, almost two years after your graduation, homeless!"

"I have an apartment, mom," objected Samantha.

"Oh no, my dearest. You call that closet an apartment?"

Samantha sighed, already getting irritated.

"Listen, Sam, I know you've always fantasized about how perfect your life would be in a fabulous city, but things don't always turn out the way you want. You can come back home any time, you know . . ."

"I'd rather die than listen to your mockery all day long," Samantha thought. There was no way she would go back to her hometown.

"No thanks, mom. I'm happy where I am. Take care of yourself."

To avoid uttering inappropriate words, Samantha had to end the conversation. With her hand on her head, she remembered her childhood dream of being a successful upperclass lady. Despite her being intelligent and hardworking, she was far from having accomplished that goal.

On getting to her tiny apartment, she remembered her mother's words describing it as a closet. Seeing the old-fashioned clothes in her wardrobe brought back the bitter taste of Claire's unpleasant remarks:

"Nice outfit, Samantha! Did you get it at a garage sale like yesterday's gown?"

"I guess if your life was a book, the title would be *Samantha the Scarecrow!*"

"I think you should write an article in the firm's journal on where to find the cheapest clothes on the planet!"

Samantha could hear the annoying laughter that accompanied each of Claire's mean sentences.

"There's got to be something I can do to get back at that vixen!" the young woman thought, enraged.

She was still lost in her thoughts when she received a call from an unknown number.

"Hi, is this Samantha?" asked the caller.

"Yes, how can I help you?"

"I've been told you are the church accountant, so I would like to meet you regarding an urgent matter. If you're free now, could you please tell me where you are? I'll meet you there as soon as possible."

Prudently, Samantha gave the person on the line the address of a popular fast-food chain close to her apartment and the caller told her she'd be there in the next thirty minutes.

Half an hour later, Samantha was having a milkshake at the appointment place when she saw a woman coming towards the table where she was sitting. Her face seemed familiar, but Samantha could not tell how exactly where they had met before. Recognizing Samantha, the woman smiled and sat across from her.

She introduced herself as Charlotte, a member of Pastor Luke's congregation, then jumped into what was bringing her to Samantha.

"For a while now, the Lord has been leading me to make a donation to support the church's missionaries."

She brought out a large envelope from her bag.

"They represent more than twenty years of savings," she continued. "I want you to put it in the church's treasury, but please, let it remain anonymous. Let no one, not even Pastor Luke, know that I made the donation. Will you do that for me, please?"

Samantha nodded in the affirmative and took the envelope.

"Thanks, my dear. I've got to go now. Take care!"

Perplexed, Samantha folded the envelope and put it in the purse she had taken with her. When she reached home, she took it out to count the total of what was inside, and she could not believe her eyes. She had never seen that much cash her whole life.

"If I had just one tenth of this, I'd get rid of all these old clothes," the lady said, sighing.

Realizing what she had just said, she stayed put for a few seconds to think: actually, what prevented her from taking part of that money? She and Charlotte were the only persons who knew the exact amount of the donation, and the woman had insisted that the donation be anonymous. She could just enter any sum of money in the church's treasury, and no one would ever know the initial amount!

After all, weren't they just numbers? As the person in charge of the treasury, the church leadership had full confidence in her and never doubted her figures. Besides Charlotte's envelope, she could use that trust to divert some of the money that the church was getting from offerings and donations into her pockets. The lady did not wait long before carrying out her malicious intentions.

However, she did not realize how her unhealthy desire to prove that she was not a nobody was slowly causing her to lose herself.

"No!" Luke shouted at the sight of this, not caring whether he could be heard or not. All he wanted was to express his disappointment and the numbness that came with the realization of being betrayed.

"Not Samantha!" cried the clergyman, disillusioned. Still in shock, he was not given time to process what he had just witnessed.

"Will you come with me, Luke?" He heard from the still and melodious voice.

Once more, the setting changed, and he found himself on a bridge.

5

Scandal

It was dark, and the place looked deserted at first glance. Yet, Luke heard whispers a few meters from where he was standing. When he turned to see from where the voices emanated, he saw two persons dressed in dark colors who looked like secret agents. Since he had gotten used to the fact that he could be neither heard nor seen, he approached them to hear what they were discussing. There were two men. The one on the left seemed in his mid-forties, while the other appeared younger.

"Is that all you got?" asked the first man, paying attention to what appeared to be printed pictures.

"Yes, but it is more than enough to do the job," answered the other.

"James and Shekill?" thought Luke, whose cup of surprises was already running over. "What could they be possibly doing here?"

James, the middle-aged man, was one of Luke's closest friends. They had known each other for about seven years. James was an architect, father of three, who dedicated time every week to preach on the streets. Luke had invited him several times to give a message to the church he was pastoring. Shekill on the other hand, was a former homeless man who was now assisting Luke in administering the shelter. Shekill had never been part of

Luke's congregation, and James did not visit the shelter that often. As Luke was wondering on what occasion they had met, he heard James saying: "That's what you said two years ago!"

"Trust me on this, boss. We have a weapon with us that we didn't have before," assured Shekill.

He then looked at his watch and told James, "Speaking of which, I have to meet her now."

"Okay," said James in agreement, while taking an envelope from his jacket to hand it to Shekill.

"Thanks!"

Shekill took the envelope furtively and left.

"My dear friend, if only you knew what was coming your way," James said, with a mysterious smile on his face.

The next scene that played in front of Luke was of Shekill and Josey in what Luke recognized to be Josey's apartment.

"This is your share," said Shekill, taking some bank notes from the envelope that James had handed him earlier.

"Are you kidding me? I'm the one who did all the work!" Josey protested, despising the sum of money Shekill was giving her.

"You will have double once the boss is satisfied."

"Now you're making sense!" Josey exclaimed, swiftly taking the money from Shekill's hand.

"Show me what you've got."

Josephine, who preferred to go by Josey, had been the church secretary for the past eight months. As Luke himself liked to say, it was a difficult task to take care of the administrative, relational, and spiritual aspects of the ministry all by himself. Thus, when Josey had offered to volunteer in church, he had put her in charge of managing his appointments, organizing meetings and church events, receiving and replying to the church's correspondence, and much more. Meanwhile, Jide, whom Luke was training to become a full-time pastor, was assisting him in his ministerial duties.

Josey opened her laptop and showed Shekill an article, with the title reading "Luke Stage: The Impostor."

"Luke Stage, alias Pastor Luke, is without any doubt the most influential philanthropist pastor in the metropole. With a congregation of not less than five thousand active members, a shelter and his involvement in numerous charity organizations, no wonder he has been named Person of the Year eight consecutive times. But do you really know who the charming Pastor Luke is?"

There were several pictures following the introduction, some that were really equivocal when taken out of context, others that had been photoshopped to present Luke in the worst way possible.

"Occultist, guru, pedophile, womanizer, Luke Stage is a crook pastor with a lavish lifestyle passing as a pauper."

"Intense!" commented Shekill, with a satisfied smile.

Luke felt his heart was about to stop beating, but he had not seen it all just yet.

———

The time travel screen took him to two years ago, when an article defaming him had been published in the newspaper. Shekill had started working with him at the shelter just a few months before then. Simple coincidence?

Luke had met Shekill the year before, when the latter had no place to go, and the clergyman had welcomed him at the shelter. After four months Shekill had gotten a job and a place to live, so he had left the shelter.

On one of his visits to his good friend James, Luke had shared with him that the Love Home shelter was short of staff. A few days later, James went unannounced to Luke's office and sneaked into his files to get the contacts of people who had recently left the shelter. With his mischievous plan already in mind, James knew he couldn't just take a stranger for his dirty job. He used Luke's notes to get Shekill's number and address and gave him the deal.

"Get close to him, gather as much information as you can that could take him down. Take pictures, ask questions, assemble evidence!" ordered James authoritatively.

The middle-aged man had offered to pay Shekill to become a volunteer at the shelter and carry out his hidden agenda.

"Pastor Luke has been good to me, you know," objected Shekill the first time. "And I have never seen him behaving inappropriately with anybody."

"I can pay you the equivalent of your yearly salary if you succeed."

Shekill had thought for a few minutes before accepting James's job.

"But if I may, sir, why do you want him down so bad?" asked the young man, concerned.

"That is none of your business," James replied.

And thus began their evil collaboration. Shekill had gone back to the shelter to meet Luke and offer him his help, which Luke had gladly accepted. In the meantime, Luke was meeting his good friend James at least twice a month, and they would catch up on what was happening in each other's life. Sometimes James would invite Luke to his house or for outdoor activities with his family.

"How can you be so happy when you've been single all your life?" James had once asked Luke.

Luke had laughed and replied, "First of all, I'm not *always* happy. Happiness is a feeling that largely depends on circumstances. I happen to feel sadness, anger, or worry sometimes. But I choose joy over them all! The joy that is made available through the Spirit in you. And that really has nothing to do with me being married or not."

He had taken a break and continued, "Besides, I am celibate by choice, James. If I had listened only to people's opinion, I would have been married a long time ago. You know, whatever choice of life we make, we must live by its standard."

James had nodded his head in approval. Luke always had the right word to say about everything. What had started as admiration in James's heart had quickly turned into envy. How could a man be so successful, have so much impact, yet remain casual about it? He had never heard Luke bragging about the size of his congregation, the number of people to whom he had reached out, or any other achievement.

James had had to admit to himself that he had started his street preaching out of his desire for recognition. He was an ambitious man, always looking for the next string to add to his bow. However, he had not and would probably never attain Luke's success . . . unless he took his place! If there was a scandal so big that would force Luke to step down, he would graciously offer to take his place and ensure that Luke never came back. James had thus begun to devise strategies for that to happen.

However, after months of working with the clergyman and trying to gather as many incriminating facts as possible, Shekill realized there was nothing scandal-worthy about Luke's life. But instead of backing out from the mission, he had had the brilliant idea of framing Luke. He put together a bunch of lies, half-truths, and statements taken out of their context to send anonymously to as many newspapers as possible anonymously. He described himself as someone having worked closely with Luke in the past. Although nearly all the papers refused to publish it because it lacked sufficient evidence to support its claims, the sensational magazine *The Lynx* published it the next day as their front-page story: "The Incredible Luke Stage."

It became the most popular topic in town, not so much because people believed the story, but because people were wondering who would hate the loveable Pastor Luke so much that they would invent such lies. In less than two days, the editor-in-chief of *The Lynx* received 587 letters from angry citizens demanding he tender a public apology or close down his business. Luke did not sue the magazine for defamation, but rather remained silent on the issue.

The episode produced the exact opposite of its intended outcome. Instead of falling victim to a scandal, Luke was acclaimed for not letting that incident affect his ministry. The magazine later issued an apology to Luke Stage and the general public. James was enraged at the failure of his henchman, but did not give up on his plan. He knew that sooner or later he would find the perfect way to oust Luke and assume his position.

"You haven't seen the videos yet!" replied Josey proudly.

Back in Josey's apartment, Luke looked at the computer screen in disbelief. The first video was of a frail-looking woman who could barely look straight at the camera.

"My name is Danika. About seven years ago my daughter and I were thrown out of our apartment by my boyfriend and had no place to go. Luke Stage met me on the street and offered me to stay at his shelter until I found a place of my own. The first few days were awesome but . . ."

The woman on the screen stopped and tears began filling her eyes.

"On the second week, he entered the room where my daughter and I were sleeping and forced me to have sex with him."

She stopped once more and sobbed for a while before she continued.

"I didn't have a place to go. I was hopeless, and he had been helping me, so I gave in reluctantly. Some days after, I went out for a walk and when I came back, my daughter, who was just eleven years old by then, told me he had abused her while I was outside! When I confronted him, all he said was that we owed him our lives."

"Who is this woman?" asked Shekill, shocked.

"Danika Malt," answered Josey. "Part of her story is true. She lived at the Love Home a couple of years back. I went to look for her three days ago, and it turns out her life is a mess. She agreed to do this, because she would do anything for a bit of money in her condition."

"Aren't we all doing this for money?"

"I have my own reasons," replied Josey, opening the next video.

Shekill wondered what reason other than money was motivating his accomplice.

———————

Meanwhile, Josey's motives were revealed on the screen before Luke's eyes.

"One year! A whole year that I'm dying for him and all he can see in me, is a sister!"

In the scene playing before Luke, Josey had just left the church building, enraged. Sitting down in her car, she remembered how she had offered to become the church secretary with the sole motive of getting close to the lead pastor. Yes, she was in love with Luke. She had turned down many suitors because she was waiting on him. Of course, she knew about his decision to remain celibate, but she always believed it was just because he had not found the right woman. She thought she could make him change his mind.

"What an idiot I've been! He has never even looked at me just once!"

She had tried almost everything to draw his attention to her, but he seemed completely blind. The worst part was that she had no rival. If only there were another woman for whom Luke had eyes, the battle would have been an easier one to win. But there was absolutely no one in whom Luke was romantically interested, and that infuriated Josey the more.

When James and Shekill resumed their evil scheme, Shekill knew he needed another one of Luke's close collaborators to succeed this time. Shekill did some research and found that, professionally, Jide and Josey were the closest persons to Luke. Since Jide's union to Elise had made him a wealthy man, there was no way he would accept joining their team for money. That left only Josey, the church secretary whom Shekill had met on a few occasions. After seeking a raise from James on the premise that he needed to bring in the heavy artillery, Shekill purposed to offer the deal to Josey. And it turned out, she was easier to convince than he had expected.

Josey actually saw in the upcoming scandal the hoped-for opportunity she had been seeking. After everyone would have turned their backs against Luke, she would offer to heal his wounds, and he would finally see all the love she had for him. How could a man resist a loyal woman in his darkest time?

"I'm in," Josey had replied, without letting Shekill finish his explanation.

She had a deep smile on her face, thinking how all this would benefit her. Shekill was surprised to see her yielding so easily, but he did not read too much into it. To him, she was in it for the money, just as he was.

———⌒———

Josey clicked on the next item, and a video of Samantha started playing on the screen.

"When I started living at Luke's shelter, he forced me to attend his church, which I must say is more of a sect. He collects money from the congregation members to support associations which do not even exist! Working at the church treasury, I found out that more than half of the money he takes from people is kept in secret bank accounts abroad. I recently discovered he owns two houses, yet he pretends to live in a rented apartment paid for by the church."

Images illustrating the declarations made by Samantha were shown in the video. Even though they could have been easily downloaded from the internet, they enhanced the quality of the video and made the claims look so genuine.

"Whoa!" Shekill exclaimed in admiration.

"This is Samantha, the one in charge of the church's treasury. I caught her altering figures in the church's accounting books recently. I gave her two options. Either she make this video and earn some cash, or I expose her in the most outrageous way possible."

"You're an evil genius!" Shekill complimented, seeing that Josey had it all figured out.

"The bomb will explode Sunday after the service. I have already made all the arrangements for that. Your boss is free to come and enjoy the show live! I can assure you, this will create the most memorable church scandal of the century," Josey added, with a loud laugh.

"Enough!" Luke shouted, even though he knew none of them could hear him. He put his hand on his chest. He was out of breath.

"I can't take anymore, Lord. Is this what I gave my whole life for?"

Luke fell on the ground and closed his eyes, not willing to be taken anywhere else.

"Luke. Don't you remember?" asked the still and melodious voice.

6

The Encounter

"June 11," said the same voice.

"June 11," whispered Luke.

As he kept his eyes shut, scenes of the past began playing in his mind.

———— ⁀ ————

It was May 29, 1994. Luke saw a much younger version of himself. He was about to turn sixteen, to be precise. It was the day that his dad passed away, two weeks before his birthday. Whenever he cast his mind back to that period, it always brought bittersweet memories to him: bitter, because his dad was the closest person to him back then; sweet, because it brought back to mind his first encounter with the Most High, the one who revealed to him the part he had to play in God's agenda.

Luke's family was as ordinary as any family in a small town. His mom Helena managed the local coffee shop, and his dad Tom was a gym instructor and coach of the basketball team in their town. Luke was their only child. One day, Tom went out for his morning jog, and an aneurysm ruptured. Before the emergency medical team arrived, he was gone. It was later revealed that he had a congenital heart defect that had started manifesting just a few years before his demise.

Luke was devastated, and so was his mother. He would often isolate himself and deeply reflect on the meaning of life. His father had been a Christian who believed everything happened for a reason. He had constantly reminded him that no one's coming to the world was a mistake, that everyone was part of God's plan and purpose. But Luke had never seen himself other than just ordinary. And apart from being a great dad, he did not see anything special about Tom either. So, what could be that purpose that he was referring to often time?

Sooner than he thought, Luke found the answer to his question in the most unexpected way. The day before his sixteenth birthday, the eleventh day of the month of June, his mother knocked at his door with a box in her hands.

"Hi, sweetie!" she said with a faint smile.

"Hi, mom," he replied with a blank expression.

"I was going through some of your dad's stuff and I found this, with your name on it."

Luke looked at his mother, surprised. She took something from the box she was holding and handed it to him. It was a DVD on which was written "My Beloved Son Luke."

"You may want to see what's on it," said his mom.

She placed the box on his table and left.

Luke went to the living room to put the DVD in the player, and a few seconds later, he saw the image of his dad projecting on the screen.

"Hi, Lukey boy. I used all my savings to buy this recorder, so it better be working . . ."

The young man smiled. This was a typical made-by-Tom icebreaker.

"Lukey, I would have loved to have this conversation with you just on your sixteenth birthday. But if you see this, it means I didn't make it till then."

He breathed in and out before continuing.

"As much as your mom and I love you with all our hearts, we can't always be there for you. But there's Someone who loves you even more than we do and who promised to always be with you. I met him a couple of years ago and he didn't just change my life, he literally gave me his!"

A bright smile illuminated Tom's face on the screen.

"He taught me how to love your mother and you just the way he does, how to consider and help others like he does, how to accept his genuine friendship and trust him completely. This purpose I always tell you about—it is in him that I discovered it. Lukey, I may not leave you much money in my bank account, but if there is just one thing that I would want you to take from my existence, it is him!"

Luke couldn't know then whether or not it was an illusion, but at that moment he had seen his father's face on their small TV screen becoming radiant and had heard his voice becoming deeper than before.

"All it takes is to respond to the love of God manifested through Jesus Christ, receive his life, and discover how you are part of his purpose."

"How do I do that?" asked Luke, his eyes full of tears.

It was not the first time for him to hear these words, but the truth is, they had never made as much sense as they did at that moment. Unknown to him, his mother had been standing a few meters behind him all this while. When she heard him ask that question, she came closer and sat on the sofa next to him.

She reminded him how God loved not just him but every single one on earth. How he knew people even before they were formed in their mother's womb, because he was their Maker. She told him about God's desire of fellowship with human beings and also about the free will that he had given them. That freedom of choice had been exercised the wrong way and had led humans to be separated from God.

"You see, Luke, men have always looked for ways to reach God," she continued. "But the only way has been given by God himself, and there is nothing to add to it."

She told him that God's love and desire to fellowship with human beings had never been altered, even in their wrong exercise of their free will. That is why he chose to write their wrongs off and start afresh.

"Christ's sacrifice was a message of love from God to mankind, a way of telling us he had always been willing and ready to accept us, and there was no longer anything holding us back. Do you believe it, sweetie?"

"I do," answered Luke.

"Then tell him you do."

Luke closed his eyes and made a prayer from the depth of his heart.

"Lord, I believe in you. I believe you know me, you made me, you love me, and have never given up on me. I may not understand it fully, but I know that the sacrifice of Jesus reconciled us with you. I say yes to your life, your friendship, to your leadership, and to your purpose."

When he opened his eyes, he saw his mother smiling at him. She took him in her arms and prayed for him.

"I have the feeling you will have a special birthday gift this year," said his mother after the prayer.

"Mom, I already told you not to bother about my birthday this year," he protested, thinking his mom would have used all her money to buy him the scooter of his dreams.

"Who said it will be from me?" asked his mom, laughing.

She got up and went towards the kitchen. Not giving it too much thought, Luke went back to his room. His attention was drawn by the box that his mom had left on his table earlier, and he saw that there was a book inside. After taking it from the box, he opened to the first page and read "My Purpose Journal" written in what he recognized as his father's handwriting.

"Revealing Christ in the world of sports" was the phrase underneath the capitalized title. In this journal, Tom was recording all his goals and successes as a Christian and main coach of the local basketball team. However, it was not done in a Dear Journal kind of way. Tom was setting objectives and recording his achievements towards their accomplishments. But they were not ordinary sports objectives, like winning the coming season or beating the next opponent. They looked more like this:

> September 22: Share the love of Christ with Josh and Andrew, newcomers to the team.
> Josh, 18, has just finished high school and is taking a gap year before college.
> Andrew, 16, lives with his single mom who brought him to the team to make new friends.
> September 25: I paid a visit to Andrew's mom to have a one-on-one with her and Andrew. I led his mom to Christ. Andrew is still hurt by his father's actions and said he does not want to have anything to do with God. I prayed with them before leaving.
> September 29: Josh received Christ today after the team's training! He asked if he could pray at the beginning of our next session.
> September 30: Kalil, Mateo, and Richard approached me today and expressed their desire to grow in their knowledge of Christ. Will it be proper to start a Bible study with the team? Lord, lead me.
> October 3: I say YES to You, Father! Pastor Joshua's message about answering God's calling hastily made me realize I have no time to waste. I will seek authorization from the teens' parents to start a Bible study with them as soon as possible.

Luke was amazed. He now understood why all the former and present members of the town's basketball team were so emotional at his father's funeral. Not only did his father pray for each of them, but he also had always sought ways to show them love and help them grow in their faith. Many had gone to college and impacted their schoolmates with the Word that had been planted in their hearts by Tom. The adults of the team had testified to having become better fathers, husbands, employees, businessmen, and so much more, thanks to Tom's impact.

Luke had thought it was not possible for his father to have achieved all that—that it was just a way for those testifying to say that Tom was a good man. However, before his eyes was the proof of his father's impact. Tom was a man who had understood the part he had to play in God's purpose and chosen to walk in it. Tears filled Luke's eyes at that very moment, but at the same time, an immense joy took over his heart to know that his father had had a life so well spent.

"I wanna be like you, dad," he said to himself. "I want to be a part of God's purpose."

Luke fell asleep with his dad's purpose journal in his hands. That night, he had a dream he would never forget. He found himself in a field with extremely large proportions. A few meters from him were a herd of sheep that were grazing. One of the sheep was far from the herd and looking unwell. He approached it and bent down to figure out what was wrong.

"If only I knew how to help you," he said to the sheep.

"You could give him some water," he heard behind him.

He turned and saw a man coming in his direction, carrying a lamb that he was feeding. The man had the majesty of a king and the simplicity of a shepherd. He smiled at Luke and asked him, "Luke. Do you want to help me look after them?"

Luke smiled timidly and nodded in the affirmative. He watched as the man tended the flock, calling them by their names, and paying attention to the needs of each sheep. At one point, he turned to Luke and asked him to do the same. The young Luke followed the man's approach and before he knew it, he knew all the sheep by name, what they needed, and how to tend them.

"Now go and keep doing it," was what the man told him before leaving.

He woke up the next morning when his mother knocked at his door with a cupcake to wish him happy birthday. After the wishes and the prayer, he told his mom about the strange dream he had had the night before. Helena smiled and told her son, "I told you that you would have a special gift this year."

"What do you mean, mom?" Luke asked, confused.

His mom told him that he had seen the King of kings and had been entrusted with his life mission.

"But . . . why didn't I see him seated on his throne, with angels around him?" Luke asked, perplexed.

Helena laughed and replied, "God's ways are so diverse, sweetie. Jesus didn't come to earth with an army and some ostentatious apparatus. He was born in a manger as the earthly son of a carpenter. Yet he was and is the King of kings! How was the man you saw?"

"He was . . . majestic but so humble. Considerate, compassionate, and a pretty good teacher."

With a bright smile on her lips, his mom hugged him. "Thank you, Father, for the good works you have prepared in advance for Luke. May he discover them and walk in them. In Jesus's name, amen."

Luke later on understood from books and interactions with other believers that he was called to what was known as the mercy ministry. Therefore, as far back as his late teenage years, his life had become all about identifying others' needs and helping them in the name of the Lord Jesus Christ. It was also around that time that he had decided not to get married. His choice of celibacy could not be said to have stemmed from a heartbreak, as he had never been in a relationship. Neither could it have come from a fear to replicate his parents' mistakes, as his parents had a happy marriage, for all he could remember. It was safe to say that he just never felt the desire to ever be in a relationship and had found fulfilment in accomplishing his God-given assignment.

After high school, Luke took a year off and undertook a missionary trip to another country, with his mother's blessing. Their local church had sent him along with the evangelism team to share the love of Christ in different regions and villages of that country. There, Luke had understood the practical sense of service to others: building boreholes, administering first aid, educating children, and so much more, not to mention preaching the Word of God to both welcoming and hostile audiences. Luke had returned to his country with a deep understanding of the word sacrifice, and that had been his mindset in ministry since then: giving his all.

"I've always given my all, wherever I was sent by you!" Luke said, feeling wronged. Has my ministry been useless all this while?

"Will you stop because of them, Luke?" was all that the voice asked him.

Even though Luke kept his eyes shut, he began hearing voices. Tens, dozens, hundreds of voices assailed his ears. From where could they possibly be coming?

7

Thoughts of the Heart

WHEN LUKE CONCEDED TO opening his eyes, he was lying on the carpet of the church's conference room. He sat up and saw that around the big table located at the center of the room were seated the church leaders, those he considered his co-workers. From the expression on their faces, they seemed to be having a crisis meeting.

"This is getting out of hand," Lawrence, the project committee manager, was saying.

"The number of congregation members has considerably increased these past two years, but what will happen when they open their eyes to who their pastor is?" Jessica asked.

"He seems to care more about his shelter than the church," Allan continued.

"I told him many times that he needed a woman to take care of him. He keeps holding to that eunuch lifestyle of his!" Carole exclaimed.

"Other pastors are building mega churches with high-tech equipment. All he cares about is giving to the needy," Lawrence said again.

"He totally refuses to follow the trend!" Solange exclaimed. "From his lifestyle to his messages, everything about him is outdated."

"God knows what he is doing with all the money this church receives in donations," Martina complained, rolling her eyes. "He's not even able to dress elegantly or get a new car!"

"He deals with families and does not even have one," Jide said. "Is he really fit to occupy this position?"

Luke saw how each of them had been sharing those same concerns with other members of the congregation, sometimes in the guise of prayer requests. The voices he heard were the rumors and the gossip that his own ministry partners were spreading. He could not believe that the ones whom he thought were sharing his vision were actually busy destroying his work with their tongues. The purpose of their Saturday meetings and leaders' retreats was to remind them of the direction in which the church was going, how they were to be part of it, and for them to express their opinion. None of these complaints had he ever heard from them, neither at a meeting nor in private.

He shook his head in disappointment and went out of the conference room, dejected. However, he was still hearing voices. He figured out that the noise was coming from the church's main auditorium and went to see what it was about. He saw the members of his congregation, all seated down and conversing. He took a walk through the steps of the main aisle, which separated the right from the left rows of the auditorium. As he walked past the front seats, he realized something strange: he could see through the people who were in the seats.

It started when he saw a speech bubble popping from Octavio's head as he was speaking with his wife Jeanine: "My wife considers me the best man who ever lived. But how would she react if she became aware that I stole my former partner Henry's business idea and never gave him credit for that? What would be my children's reaction if they knew I hired hitmen to assassinate Henry to make sure he'd never claim anything from me? They all think I pay for his children's school fees because I'm a good man, but it's all out of guilt."

His wife Jeanine also had a bubble that appeared above her forehead: "Octavio thinks that all I need is money and does not care about my other needs! I'm so desperate for affection that I've started dating our son's best friend. How long will I be able to keep this a secret?"

Luke turned to the right and saw Therese, who was smiling and nodding her head while Yasmine, seated next to her, was speaking. He could see Therese sighing internally and thinking: "Just because I'm a middle-aged woman and a so-called church counselor doesn't mean I have to listen to these people's marital struggles! The only reason I indulge them is because I so much like using their weaknesses against them, without them ever finding out . . ."

Luke was able to see how much of a manipulator Therese was. She had turned men against their wives and had instilled rebellion in the hearts of women through her consciously wrong pieces of advice. She had equally caused the end of some friendships in the congregation by inappropriately sharing confidential information she to which she had access as a counselor.

On the row just behind them, Prisca, one of the worship team's lead singers, was humming with her headphone on. She received a notification that she had been tagged on a picture posted by a famous cabaret in town. She quickly removed the tag before it appeared on her followers' feed. She had posted countless pictures on her social media accounts of her ministering in church with captions like "I Sing Only for Jesus" or "My Heart Is All His." How would she look like if it was discovered that she was regularly performing in a non-Christian setting? To keep it secret, she always made sure that she would not be recognized while singing at a cabaret. She was usually performing with a wig and contact lenses or sunglasses, under a pseudonym. Up to now, nobody had ever confronted her about her double-dealing, and she intended to keep things that way.

A few seats away from her, George was discussing work ethics with Cassandra, a recent graduate who had just landed her first job.

"Integrity and loyalty are the key," he was saying. "Do not be concerned about the money, it will come along the way."

As Cassandra was taking down notes, George bit his lip over his last words. He had been selling his company's business secrets to their biggest competitor and making false entries in the company's books for about three years now. How ironic was it for him to be lecturing someone on integrity!

On another row, Peter and Katy were planning on how to make the coming Easter celebration memorable for the children of the orphanage they were supporting. But they failed to realize that they had become total strangers to their own children, Naya and Kevin. Aged fourteen and sixteen respectively, the teenagers were battling with gambling, drug, and porn addictions under their parents' noses. Peter and Katy were so busy giving attention to other kids that they completely forsook theirs.

Luke saw dozens of bubbles popping from other members of the congregation revealing their well-guarded secrets, until he could not bear it any longer. Feeling like his heart had been replaced by a hundred-pound weight, he bowed his head and allowed tears to roll down his face. His eighteen years of faithful service in God's vineyard had yielded a bunch of hypocrite Christians who were no way close to Christlikeness.

Once he lifted his head, he was back in his study room.

8

The Good Shepherd

THAT NIGHT WAS CERTAINLY the most horrible in Luke's existence. The last time he had cried this hard was after his father's demise. But the realization of his failure in his life mission was comparable to, if not greater than, the loss of a loved one. He had never been after people's approval and certainly did not expect everyone to love him, but seeing the closest persons to him betraying him was disheartening. Discovering that the people in whom he had invested his time and resources to nurture, teach, and train were nothing they pretended to be was devastating. Wasn't he a teacher of the truth? Wasn't he practicing what he was preaching? Was he not praying for them? Was he not giving his all? What was he not doing right?

Luke stayed awake until Sunday morning, his heart heavier than the night before. He had not heard the Holy Spirit speaking to him anymore, and Luke wondered if all the scenes that had played before him a few hours back were what he meant by, *"Do you know Love?"* But that did not matter anymore, as Luke had decided not to deliver the last part of his message on love.

Gathering all the strength he had left, he prepared to go to church. All through the 9.7 miles that separated his house from the church, he kept gritting his teeth and driving with his hands firmly gripping the steering wheel. Once he reached the building, he went straight to his office and put out his "Do not disturb" sign for nobody to knock at his door. With his head in his hands testifying to his powerlessness, Luke stayed in his office until the end of the praise and worship session, which was unlike him.

When he finally came out, he climbed directly on the pulpit, carrying neither his Bible nor his notebook. He rather had a somber look with which no one had ever seen him. He had already prepared his speech. He planned to tell them how disappointing it was to lead a congregation of liars, cheats, traitors, crooks, and hypocrites. He was ready to expose all the sins they had spent so much time covering up. Indeed, when he looked at each of them, all he could see was the deepest dark of their souls.

More than four minutes had passed, and Luke was still standing behind the pulpit without having uttered a single word. He was giving the congregation a cold and fixed look and had been maintaining a firm posture. When he saw Therese whispering to George about their pastor's strange demeanour, he clenched his fist and tried not to remember the havoc she had been creating between members of the congregation. Not far from Therese and George, Roger was holding Stephanie's hand affectionately, faithful to their perfect family image ideal. Luke couldn't help but have a spasm of disgust when he recalled that they had been putting on a show all this while.

As Luke's eyes were going from one member to another, resentment kept growing within him. He had totally ignored the signals that Jide had been sending him to find out if everything was all right. When Luke's gaze fell upon Samantha and Josey sitting at the back of the auditorium, it became fiercer. He could not hold it any longer. He had to give the aggressive speech he had prepared.

"I am . . ."

". . . announcing that I quit being your pastor!" was what he had in mind. But why was he not able to finish his sentence? Instead, he swallowed the remaining words and bowed his head, trying to gather his thoughts.

Almost immediately, Jide got up from his seat and approached the stage:

"Pastor Luke, are you okay?" Jide asked him in a low voice.

"I don't need your help," Luke replied coldly, signaling him with his hand not to approach him.

When he lifted his head, ready to give his address, he saw none of the members of his congregation. The auditorium was now looking like a vast field, and a herd of sheep was scattered all over the place. Luke heard someone humming and instinctively turned to see the man he had seen for the first time twenty-five years before. Sitting down, he was feeding one of the sheep while caressing its head, humming.

"Are you tired, Luke?" was all he asked.

"Tired?! I am frustrated, disappointed! I am feeling betrayed, useless! I spent all my life taking care of the sheep you brought my way, and this is all it amounts to?"

The man signaled to Luke that he could sit down next to him.

"You know, Luke, I went through what you're experiencing right now. I was misunderstood, betrayed, and abandoned by the people closest to me. Not to talk of those who opposed me openly and falsely accused me. Does that mean my mission was a failure?"

Luke said no with his head.

"And guess what?" the man continued, "Through it all, I never abandoned my sheep."

"But what do you do when the sheep are nothing like they ought to be, despite . . . all the resources you put in them."

"You speak to the Father about them, you keep feeding them, and most importantly, you see them with the Father's eyes."

"Father's eyes?" asked Luke, intrigued.

"Look around you," the man said.

Suddenly, the sheep that were scattered and looking feeble when Luke first saw them, were now men and women all gathered in one place, radiant, blameless, and strong.

"The Father loves all his sons and daughters, and we see them as we created them to be. It does pain us to see them unaware of who they really are and not functioning as such. Thus, we send shepherds to help them grow in the knowledge we have of them. That is what we mean by feeding them. No matter the number of mistakes the sons and daughters make, we never give up on them and do not define them by their wrongdoings."

"But . . . what if they keep doing the same mistakes over and again! How long are we to feed them?"

"Until everything about them reflects their nature and identity as sons and daughters of the Most High."

Luke remained quiet.

"When I met you twenty-five years ago, did I tell you how long it would take?" the man asked him.

At first Luke did not say a word, pondering over his first encounter.

"But . . . why did you show me all their flaws! How do you expect me to look at them or lead them the same way now?"

The man laughed heartily. "Luke, you asked to be taught about love, remember?"

The clergyman shook his head in the affirmative, wondering what his message on love had to do with all he had witnessed in the previous hours.

"Our love is perfect, absolute, unconditional. It is not based on rumors, perceptions, conditions, not even facts, and all other barriers created by human reasonings. It is not stopped by feelings, no matter how hurtful they may be. We are all-knowing, so what you witnessed last night, we see it all the time. But why do we keep loving?"

Luke was beginning to understand the uneasiness he had had in relation to his message. He had yet to fully grasp the truth of God's love.

"Because, son, our love for our creation never runs dry."

When the man pronounced the last words, Luke suddenly felt like a river of water had formed in his belly and was flowing in and from his chest. He looked down at his body to figure out what was happening to him, but nothing was seen on the outside.

"That same inexhaustible love has already been poured out in your heart. All you need is to express *him*."

"All you need is to express him . . . all you need is to express him."

As the man's words kept sounding in his ears, Luke's heart began beating faster than usual. Looking around him, he realized he was no longer in the vast field.

9

The Message of Love

WITH HIS LEFT HAND, Luke wiped the droplets of perspiration on his forehead, while his right hand was placed on his chest. He was down on one knee, breathing heavily. He could not tell how many minutes had passed, but he did know that all the sadness, disappointment, anger, and disdain he was feeling before had completely vanished.

It was the voices of his congregation members that brought him back to reality. Actually, he had been in a trance for barely five minutes, but the members had seen his face turning in an instant from aggressive to expressionless and had witnessed his body going down on one knee without him uttering a single sound.

Luke's eyes blinked multiple times as he was recovering from his encounter. When he turned his head to the right, Jide had climbed the pulpit and was looking at him anxiously, wondering what he had to do. When he noticed that Luke now seemed lucid, he came closer and asked, "Pastor Luke, do you need some help?"

Luke looked up in his direction and gave him a smile. Then he gave Jide his right hand for him to help him get up.

"Thanks, Jide. I'm fine, don't you worry."

He gave him a tap on the shoulder and told him he could go back to his seat. Then, he took the mic and faced his audience.

"Good morning, everyone. I am sorry if I somewhat scared you earlier on. I was . . . perfecting my sermon."

All the people present gave him a look of surprise, asking themselves if his preaching had to do with stage performances, because of the numerous expressions he had had in just a few minutes.

"The message I'm about to give you has nothing to do with what I had prepared for this morning."

To be honest, he did not know exactly what he was going to tell his congregation, but he was certain that neither the third part of his love series nor his aggressive address were what he had to deliver.

"Father, I pray you speak to your sons and daughters. In Jesus's name, amen."

After praying, he felt uncomfortable standing in the pulpit as usual and decided to go down. Definitely, the lead pastor's behavior was more than strange this Sunday.

"Permit me to leave my pedestal for today and stand at the same level with all of you."

He gave them a smile and continued, ready for a heart-to-heart.

"When I started this series about love two weeks ago, my goal was to make you understand or remind you how to express love, using my experience as an example. I shared with you countless genuine stories of giving, counseling, sheltering, serving, offering second chances.

"You see, I never thought I could get tired of loving. In more than eighteen years of serving others, I did experience hurt, rejection, frustration, and the like, but that never kept me from reaching out to more people. So, I felt what more than my experience would teach you the way to love? But just recently, I realized how wrong I was."

He observed a pause, as though he was carefully choosing his words.

"If one considers love as a standard of behavior to maintain, or as a set of expectations from one's self and others, one is on the wrong track. Because we all fall short of standards sometimes, and people won't always meet our expectations. If we see things through that lens, that means we would simply stop loving them when that happens. Or we might think we continue to love people, whereas we'll look out for their next wrongdoing to nail them in our hearts.

"I realized that I was wrong to have shown you, from a human perspective, what is divine. Love is who God is. It is not just an attribute of his, it is his nature. He loves because he is. And there is nothing that can stop him from loving you and me, not even ourselves.

"Believe me, God is aware of our brokenness. He knows that unfaithfulness, that greed, jealousy, betrayal, pretence, scheming, backbiting, disloyalty, and all the secrets we strive to hide, sometimes even from our very selves. Nothing is hidden from him!"

It was clear that upon hearing their flaws being pointed out so bluntly, many of the members started feeling uneasy. However, as they quickly realized, Luke's message wasn't about them.

"But I want to tell you that his love is the lens through which he looks at us, the only criterion he uses in defining us. We may think that we are not enough for that too good to be true kind of love, but the more we feel unworthy of his love, the wider his affectionate arms are open to receive us . . ."

The congregation's hearts were moved not just by their pastor's words, but also by the glorious presence of the Almighty God that had filled the atmosphere.

"I'm not worthy of his love!" shouted a lady seated on the fifth row to the left of the hall, with her voice full of emotion.

Luke turned his head to where the sound was coming from and saw Laetitia, a woman who had started attending services just recently.

She stood up, her eyes filled with tears. "I am a homewrecker! I was . . . abused by my uncle under my father's nose."

Her upper body trembling, she continued, "I grew up hating men and family! I've only dated married men to take them away from their wives and children. I pretended to be a Christian and attended churches to target those Christian men who think they are better than the rest of men. I took pleasure in tearing down homes!"

She stood silent for a moment, then asked with a shaking voice: "How could I be worthy of his love?"

Laetitia wept aloud, and for a few seconds, the audience was as quiet as a graveyard. Such a spontaneous reaction to a message had never happened during their well-organized services.

Pastor Luke walked to where Laetitia was standing, helped her wipe her tears, and gave her a warm hug.

"He still loves you," he told her softly.

Since his mic was still on, the whole congregation heard his words and were shocked. Not because they had never heard that sentence before, but because it felt more real when pronounced after such a heart-wrenching confession.

After Laetitia had calmed down, Luke returned to the front of the auditorium. With a reassuring tone, he resumed speaking to the congregation.

"I want you to picture your earthly parents or those who might have played that role in your life. You may have found flaws in the way they expressed their love to you, and this might even have affected the way you perceive God's love. Say, for instance, that your parents scolded you whenever you brought bad grades home and rewarded you when you scored good grades, it is possible you viewed your relationship with God the same way, that is, solely dependant on your good or bad behavior and your performance. Or, if your parents weren't present for you when you needed them most, it is possible you see God as a faraway being who only handles important matters and does not have time for your boring life. Again, people who experienced hurt or rejection from their parents could see no reason in trusting a God who may fail them.

"Well, let me tell you that if the perception you have of him is based on a human model, it is likely untrue. Not to say that humans are too imperfect or don't reflect God's nature, that isn't the point. The point is, there comes a time when you must learn to know God for who he is, and not only for what you have heard about him. You must understand the depth and perfection of his love for you."

"That same love that knew you before the earth was made, that chose you before you existed. That love that has always longed to fellowship with you and is ready to climb mountains, dive into the deepest oceans, pull down all obstacles on the way, just to be with you. Yes, you! The love that is never too busy for you, that cannot reject you; the One who promised to never leave you, nor forsake you. That love that gave his very self to make sure you are his eternally. That love that cost so much, but was given freely.

"He took the risk of loving us even when we could not return it. In the midst of what the human eye may consider ugly, that love sees beauty. He does not call us by our mistakes."

Luke could see the masks of his audience gradually falling from their faces. The lies and pretences they had held onto for so long were being progressively torn down by the truth of God's love.

"Brethren, God's love transcends the wrong image that we— or others around us—have of who we are. Whether it is that feeling of helplessness which pushes us to compromise our true identity, or that desire to prove ourselves to the world that slowly takes over our lives, it all starts with a wrong conception about one's self.

"It's not just about the feeling that what we have is not enough. It's about the false belief that *we* are not enough. No matter the name we give to it in order to justify our actions, we know when it is unhealthy. You and I know exactly when our next achievement comes from the desire to *feel* complete. We know how it pushes us to do anything whatsoever, simply because we believe we will find fulfilment in it.

"You see, whatever we achieve outside of his love makes us weary. But so often, we make the mistake of thinking that the next project, contract, relationship, position, title, will place a roof over the house of completeness we are building—which obviously is not true.

"I am not saying we won't aim at anything! But we must constantly remind ourselves that what we aim at and even what we already have, do not define us, neither do they make us complete.

Being conscious of and resting in His unfailing love, are what give us the greatest satisfaction."

The preacher looked at the congregation, who was deeply moved by the message, and told them:

"God's infinite love made you complete, whole, blameless, through the death, resurrection, and triumph of Jesus Christ. His Word says that he made you heir of the same heritage as Christ. If you see yourself as God sees you, you won't have to compromise to obtain what he has already given to you, neither would you live your life to receive the honor of men. When you acknowledge his perfect love, you begin to express that very nature of his, because 'It is Christ who lives in you' (Galatians 2:20). You allow him who lives in you to love others and your own self through you.

"And all this becomes your reality when you respond to his love . . ."

As Luke was still speaking, he saw Stephanie Lynn standing up from where she was sitting and walking straight to the front, with tears filling her eyes. She knelt down and placed her hands on the altar, sobbing. At that moment, she cared less about preserving her image as the calm and collected Mrs. Lynn, who exhibited happiness, self-control, and elegance in all circumstances. She was also not concerned about her pact with her husband to be the model wife at all times. She was ready to tear down the castle of deceit she had built with her own hands.

Though Pastor Luke was shocked by Stephanie's spontaneous reaction, he kept speaking to his audience.

"Repentance is your response to God's extravagant love and grace. It's choosing to let go of that wrong image of God, of yourself, and of others that you've held on to for so long. It's renouncing that burdensome life you've lived outside of Christ and receiving his life, his fullness! It's constantly renewing your mind to see all, I mean all things, just as he does . . ."

By the time Luke finished his last sentence, he heard voices, sounding like a multitude, rising from the church auditorium. On their knees, from their seats, standing or walking towards the altar, all the members were lifting up their voices, in response to the love to which the eyes of their hearts had just been opened.

10

It's Not Over Yet

"For these reasons, I believe I am not worthy of this position . . ."

Jide was sitting in Luke's office, his head bowed in shame. It was the Friday after Luke's overwhelming message on love, and the young man had spent the hardest week of his life. In response to his fresh understanding of God's love, he had decided to abandon his double-dealing, but that was not an easy task. Even though he was willing to make things right with his wife, he had gotten so involved with Solange that he did not know how to end their affair.

Jide had spent sleepless nights and had barely eaten the whole week. On many occasions he had wanted to sit his wife down and pour out his heart to her, but he just could not summon the courage to. Exhausted, he had decided it was time to let go of that burden and come clean, at least before one of the people he respected the most.

Luke had listened attentively to Jide's confessions, which were matching exactly what he had seen on the time travel screen less than a week ago. He made sure not to interrupt the young man a single time and only nodded his head once in a while to signify that he was paying attention. Jide had finished his monologue by tendering his resignation from the position of assistant pastor.

"Do you think it's the right thing to do?" asked Luke with a calm tone.

"To be honest with you, pastor, I don't know what to do anymore. Your message last Sunday made me realize how self-centered I have been all my life. Even my decision to serve as your assistant was taken with the wrong motives. I'm yet to understand how to love and serve God and others, starting with my wife . . ."

Luke smiled inwardly upon hearing the last segment of Jide's sentence.

"Do you remember the first lesson of our pre-marital counseling sessions?" He asked the young man.

"God, my spouse, and others," Jide replied.

"Correct. Following the principles of that lesson, I will advise you to first pour out your heart to the Father. You've understood so much from him lately, and it definitely shook your world. But you haven't responded yet. I know how much fear can prevent you from communicating with him, but rest assured that he will not reject you. Then, as scary as it can be, you will have to speak with your wife. Not only do you owe that to her, but keeping it to yourself will not help your marriage. And I am sorry to say this, but you must respect whatever decision she will take after you will have spoken. Finally, you will need to confront Solange."

Jide looked at his pastor in shock. How did he know she was the one? He had been careful not to mention her name in his narrative nor disclose the fact that she was a member of their local church.

Ignoring Jide's surprised gaze, Luke offered to pray for the young man before releasing him.

"Thank you, Pastor Luke."

Luke smiled as he watched the young man leave his office. His past few days had been filled with countless phone calls, messages, and visits from those who had heard his message on God's love.

It had all started with James, who had attended the church service that Sunday with the sole intent of watching the videos Josey had prepared to project immediately after Luke's preaching, both in the church's auditorium and on online platforms. Needless to say, the glorious atmosphere during the service had not only crushed their plan for good, but had also exposed and expunged the selfish desires that had made them devise such a strategy in the first place.

"How could I have ever harbored those thoughts in my heart?" James asked himself that Sunday morning. Down on his knees, he realized the extent to which he was ready to go to satisfy his fleshly ambitions. "I so much wanted to prove to myself and even to God, that I was better than others, that I looked down on my part in God's plan . . ." He said to himself, remorseful.

James had rushed into Luke's office after the service and confessed to all that had gone through his mind for the past two and a half years, as well as his plot to discredit Luke in order to take his place.

"I would fully understand if you wanted me out of your life," James concluded, having his head between his hands, weeping silently.

Luke remained quiet for a while. The truth was, he had never gone through such betrayal, probably because he did not have that many close friends. This made him realize how much the deepest wounds are indeed caused sometimes by the closest relationships. From a human perspective, the right thing to do would have been to cut ties with James. Was it not often said that even the purest love forgives but never forgets? However, on Saturday, March 21, Luke had understood like never before that love was not what he had thought it to be.

"You see them through the Father's eyes . . ."

This portion of his conversation with the King of kings came flashing at him. And a scripture he knew all too well rose in his heart:

Love "does not dishonor others, it is not self-seeking, it is not easily angered, it keeps no record of wrongs" (1 Corinthians 13:5).

It keeps no record of wrongs.

"Honestly, I don't know what to say, Father. Please, love through me," Luke said inwardly.

Less than a minute later, he lifted his head, looked intently at James, and opened his mouth to speak, although not knowing exactly what he would say.

"I forgive you, James," the clergyman finally declared with a calm and comforting tone.

This simple but heartfelt assertion was coming from his innermost part, and Luke secretly marveled at how an apparently simple prayer had taken away the uneasiness he had been feeling while listening to James's confession.

In shock, James let down his hands that had been covering his tearful face and gave a befuddled look to the man facing him.

"I . . . Thank you, Luke . . ." he managed to say.

He sniffed and continued speaking in a shattered voice.

"In all the years I've been a Christian, I've just realized how much my life has been based on performance. You know, I felt good knowing that everything about me, including the love and admiration people have for me, was earned by my own means. And the more success I had, the more worthy I felt . . . I guess that is the way I've related to God, too. I was focused on doing this stuff, you know, the street preaching and all, convincing myself I needed that to be accepted or even, approved by him . . ."

James sighed and stayed mute for about two minutes, his head lifted towards the ceiling.

"Thank you for the seed planted in my heart today, Luke," James suddenly said, with a smile.

He stood up from the guest chair in Pastor Luke's office as though he suddenly remembered he had something important to do.

"You probably won't see me around for a while, I'll be taking a break from everything . . . That boundless and amazing love you described in your sermon? I've got to discover that for myself!"

On that note, James left the room, not caring about his swollen eyes and his face full of dried-up tears. Luke's countenance was illuminated with a grin as he wished him well in his new journey.

Not only that Sunday afternoon, but throughout the days that followed, Luke kept receiving feedback on what the preaching had sparked in the lives of members of his congregation. On Friday afternoon, after meeting with Jide, he closed his office earlier than usual and jumped in his car to go pay a visit to his mother. Although they lived in different towns, Luke never spent a month without going to see her.

Helena, now sixty-nine, was still living in the house where Luke grew up. She had not remarried after Tom's death. When she was not running the local coffee shop, she was lending a helping hand to anyone around. From free babysitting and baking to teaching Sunday school in church, she never missed an opportunity to serve with a smile.

"Lukey!" She greeted happily when she saw her son opening the old-fashioned doors of her coffee shop.

Some of the customers present waved at Luke as he entered, while others left their seats to greet him with a handshake. No matter how little he had been away from his hometown, Luke was always welcomed with the same enthusiasm.

"Hi, mom," Luke replied, having walked up to the counter where Helena was standing.

"Come give me a hug and wear a uniform, young man!" Helena ordered with her sweet voice.

Laughing heartily, Luke went behind the counter, embraced his mother, and started helping her serve the customers. Soon it turned 6 p.m., and Helena placed the "Closed" sign at the door, then sat at one of the dining tables.

"You're looking good, mom," Luke complimented, handing her a cup of hot chocolate.

"Not as good as you, city boy, so stop flattering me!" she replied, signaling him to come sit beside her.

Luke dragged a chair next to hers, and they started sharing with each other about what had happened in their lives for the past few weeks.

"I finally accepted Philippe's invitation for dinner. We are going out this Saturday . . ."

"Mom!" Luke exclaimed, pleasantly surprised that Helena had given a chance to her long-time suitor.

Philippe, a widower, was the church administrator in Helena's local assembly.

"Well, I'm still praying about all that," Helena said, taking a sip of the hot chocolate.

"Definitely, you have your whole life to think about it," Luke said jokingly, causing both of them to explode in laughter.

"Enough about me," Helena said firmly. "How are you doing?"

Luke could hardly hide his excitement while talking about the revelation of love he had gotten from the Lord, how it all came about, and the testimonies he kept receiving from the members of his congregation.

"Glory be to God!" Helena exclaimed, sharing in her son's joy. "It's always refreshing to hear how the Lord is caring for his children, reminding them he's all they've ever needed . . ."

Helena turned to her son, her face shining with enthusiasm as though she suddenly remembered something good.

"Do you remember that passage in Exodus where Moses was visited by his father-in-law?" She asked.

"Yes, in Exodus 18 . . . Why?"

"Well, it came to my spirit just now," she continued. "In that passage, Moses's father-in-law was happy to hear the wonderful things that Yahweh had done for Israel, but was also worried that Moses would get tired if he kept leading the people all by himself . . . Discovering the Father's love and profound desire of fellowship with his children is a journey, and you need faithful men and women to help you lead God's children through this. You don't have to do it all alone, son. Like the apostle Paul told Timothy, you must surround yourself with people with whom you will entrust this message and who will in turn pass it across to others."

Luke sighed deeply, remembering the conversations he heard between the church leaders in the Saturday evening vision.

"To be honest, mom, I don't think the current leaders would be willing to take the responsibility of teaching others . . ."

"It doesn't have to be the formal church leadership, you know," Helene interjected. "Teaching has never been a matter of title or position, but more of a disposition of the heart to give your all to the Lord by passing on knowledge to others. That's why even the world recognizes it as a vocation."

With a touch of nostalgia, she asked her son, "Your father, what title did he have?"

Luke pondered on that for a few seconds. Even though people respectfully called his dad coach, Tom was just a sports fan who had volunteered to teach young people how to stay healthy by offering basketball classes during his spare time. While at it, he had discovered how much more God was interested in the wellbeing of their souls and spirits than simply their physical fitness. Slowly but surely, he had used every opportunity to witness the love of God to the youth he was coaching and plant seeds of the Word of Christ in their hearts.

"None," Luke answered, as in a whisper.

"Yet the testimonies of his positive impact abound till today, almost three decades after he died," Helena said, taking the last gulp of her hot chocolate. "If there is one thing your father's life taught me, it's that true leadership is not about a position, but service to God and men."

The sexagenarian got up from her seat to drop her cup in the kitchen found at the back of the shop.

"Are you spending the night, city boy?" She asked, at the top of her voice.

"No thanks, mom!" Luke answered, looking at his watch.

He quickly got up and walked over to kiss her goodbye.

"I would have loved to stay and take pictures of you and Mr. Philippe on Saturday before your date, but I've got to be at the shelter first thing tomorrow morning."

Helena chuckled when he mentioned her dinner with Philippe.

"Don't be silly, we are no longer high schoolers," she replied amused. "You better go now. They announced a heavy rain for tonight."

"Yes, ma'am," Luke answered, giving her a warm hug. "I love you, mom."

"I love you too, sweetie. Drive safe!"

After the goodbye embrace, he took his coat and car key from the hanger, waived at Helena, and left. Through the two-hour drive, the clergyman could not help but reflect on how much things had changed in his life in less than a week. He thought of how seeing members of his congregation at their weakest point had opened his eyes to how best he could provide help in feeding them. Though he felt overwhelmed by the workload it would entail, the words of wisdom spoken by his mother resonated in his heart as he pulled over into his driveway: "You don't have to do this all alone, son."

After he came out of his car, Luke went straight to the main entrance of his apartment, eager to get a good night's rest after the eventful day he had. However, he had not expected to meet someone standing at his front door, drenched by the heavy rain.

11

The Little Things

WEARING NOTHING MORE THAN a pair of jeans and a blouse, the lady was shivering. It was difficult to tell how long she had been standing there, but it was certainly long enough to be on the verge of hypothermia.

Without asking any questions, Luke quickly let her inside, offered her a chair, a clean towel, and a blanket. He went to his kitchen to boil some water to make her a cup of tea.

"Thanks, Pastor Luke," she muttered, when he handed her a cup of hot tea.

Luke raised an eyebrow, surprised to hear her call him that.

"I went to the office, but I didn't see you," she started, holding the cup of tea with both hands.

"I was at my mom's place," he replied matter-of-factly.

"I'm sorry to have come unannounced, but I really needed to speak with you . . ." The young woman continued, with an inch of gravity in her voice.

Luke sat opposite her, both hands crossed on his chest.

"Well, here am I," he said.

"Pastor Luke, I . . ."

"Josey, you've called me by my first name for as long as we've known each other," Luke interrupted. "Clearly, the formality is uncalled for."

"That's exactly what I needed to talk to you about."

Josey cleared her throat and resumed speaking, under the attentive gaze of Luke.

"I . . . fell in love with you almost the moment I saw you. I was following the Lynn family on social media and they had organized this charity event at your church. As a blogger, I'm always looking for something interesting to write on, so I decided to stop by . . . And there you were! You walked up to me that day, just like you did with everyone present, thanking them for participating. You had this genuine concern for people in your eyes, that I had never seen before . . . You didn't even need to invite me for services, I was there the next Sunday, determined to get to know you by all means. Everything I did, from calling you Luke when everyone else was calling you Pastor—not that you did mind—to getting to volunteer in church, was all a bid to draw your attention and get close to you."

For a dozen seconds, there was silence in the room. Josey bowed her head, then lifted it up toward Luke.

"Call it infatuation or what not, but the more I got to know you, even from afar, the more I wanted to be with you. I remember the first meaningful conversation we had, in your office—the new member's interview, as you called it. I already knew you weren't married, so I took the opportunity that day to ask you why . . . Your answer broke my heart, but instead of letting it go, I chose to cling to what I knew in my heart to be the impossible. I became somewhat obsessed with the idea of us being together, but it seemed like the more I did, the less you saw! And I . . . was mad at you for that. So mad that I did the unforgivable . . ."

She told him how she had become James and Shekill's ally in their attempt to defame Luke's character. Luke still had his arms crossed on his chest, carefully listening to the motivations behind Josey's actions.

"Last Sunday we were all so caught up in what happened during the service that we didn't carry on with the plan. At the end of the service, I ran outside so quickly because . . . I didn't know how to face you; I couldn't pretend any longer."

Josey paused for a second before adding:

"If it wasn't already obvious from all I've said till now, I must tell you that I've been passing off as a Christian for all the time you've known me. I mean, I saw church as a big therapy group where people were just coming to feel better about life. Some people say they don't believe in God, but I guess I was more of the indifferent type, I didn't care if he existed or not . . . Until last Sunday evening, when he called my name."

The young woman shook her head to prevent the tears that filled her eyes from flowing down.

"I was so troubled after your message that I just couldn't get home, so I began driving around town, not knowing where I was going. And, how do I say it? I heard his voice, loud and clear, as though it was coming from my heart, but at the same time, from above my head. He said, '*Josephine, I love you.*' I had never heard that voice before. I instinctively turned around to see if anybody had spoken, but obviously I was alone in my car. So, I thought I was hallucinating! But less than two minutes after, he said louder, '*Josey, you're my beloved.*' To me, there was no doubt it was him! The funny thing is, I often thought that if the God I had heard of truly existed, he must have given up on people like me already, I mean those who clearly don't care about him. The least I expected, was a declaration of love from him."

Josey chuckled. With a distant look in her eyes, it seemed she was reliving every instant she was narrating.

"I immediately went home and took my Bible, the one you offered me months ago during the newcomer's interview. Then I had taken it without having the intention of ever opening it, but there I was, rushing to it for the first time. That is how I was hooked. For the past six days, I haven't left my apartment. I've been using the 'How to Read the Bible' guide you gave me. I have also felt God leading me to some passages, and it's been amazing! I've understood how empty—or should I say filled with void?—my life has been without him. And the love I've craved? Everyday he teaches me how much I'm loved, desired by him . . ."

She looked in Luke's direction and said, "So, I've come to thank you, Pastor Luke. Even though my motives of being around you were corrupt, you kept showing me the way. In all our staff meetings, you never missed the opportunity to exhort us. I absolutely didn't like it then, but now I know that your teachings went a long way in helping me find the truth. I'll be forever grateful to God for bringing you my way."

"Wow!" Luke exclaimed, marveling at the emotional rollercoaster Josey had just described to him.

"I know it may take time to get over the feelings I've had for you, but . . . I'd like to keep coming to church, if that's okay with you. And for the volunteering, I think I'll be more helpful in another department, just so I don't make you uncomfortable, you know."

Luke laughed at her last sentence.

"Of course, you're welcome at church anytime, Josey. And feel free to serve in any department you're led to. Allow me to pray with you and call a cab for you, all right?"

Just as he had said, the clergyman joined hands with his guest and prayed for her to keep discovering the love of the Lord for her and grow in the grace and knowledge of Christ. Then, even though she insisted that she could walk back home, he called a taxi, walked her to the front door, and waved her goodbye as she was getting inside the car.

Luke got back into his apartment and went to his study room to plan the coming days, despite having no idea of what they would look like. What was certain was that, having understood that his part in God's agenda was far from being over, he had repented from the fleshly impulse to step down as lead pastor. Yet, he could not help but feel anxious of what he sensed to be ahead of him.

Closing his eyes, he muttered a prayer that rose from his heart.

"Lord, you've shown me how much you love and care about us and desire us to respond to that by fellowshipping with you. You've also reminded me how anything undertaken outside of you, whether it looks honorable or utterly wrong, is bound to fail. Even though the people whose lives you showed me were somewhat close to me, I now know that this wasn't about me, but about you. As you first told me two decades ago, I will keep feeding the ones you give me, as long as you want me to. You said I'm not alone, so I'm eagerly waiting for you to lead me through this new phase, by your Spirit. In Jesus's name, amen."

"*Start with the little things, Luke,*" the voice whispered to his heart after his prayer.

Feeling inspired, the clergyman took a pencil and a notebook, then began jotting down all that was coming to his mind.

"Happy birthday, Pastor Luke!"

Luke had just walked into the church conference room, and the least he had expected to see was a room packed full of people with bright smiles, confetti, and birthday hats. He turned towards Samantha, who was standing right behind him, and asked, "Did you know about that?"

From the knowing look on her face, he knew she must have been part of the organizing committee of the surprise celebration. Shaking his head in disbelief, Luke entered the room and was warmly greeted by the dozens of people present. He had walked in prepared to have a meeting with the church staff and volunteers, not knowing they had pulled up a feast in his honor.

Birthday parties had never been Luke's thing, not just because the period around his birthday brought back memories of his father's death, but also, he usually did not have people with whom to celebrate. However, this year was different. Luke laid an appreciative gaze on each of the persons present in the room. Some of them were people with whom he had never had a meaningful conversation just a few months ago. Today, they had become his closest collaborators.

About one year and three months had passed since Luke's sneak peek journey into the lives of some members of his congregation, and a number of little things had happened since then. With the congregation having experienced a significant increase of members for the past three years, Luke had realized how difficult it was to regularly have individual meetings with members of the church, as he desired to. He had therefore followed his mother's advice and prayerfully sought for people who would profoundly understand the new directives and assist in leading the people. He had also gone deeper into his study of the Scriptures to understand more about the love that takes away the focus from self to what matters the most.

Undoubtedly, his new discoveries impacted his sermons and counseling sessions for the better. However, he knew all too well that there was a difference between receiving a message and assimilating it, putting it into practice, and standing by it when need be. Thus, his goal became to give everyone the opportunity to listen, understand, and apply the Word. With wisdom and strategic planning, he divided up the congregation into small fellowship groups where people would feel comfortable learning, discussing, and sharing their struggles. The groups were to meet as often as they needed to outside the regular church service hours and were each appointed a lead who worked directly with Luke.

What started as an insignificant exercise slowly turned around the lives of hundreds of people. Being constantly reminded of God's love helped them overcome their struggles with self-worth, acceptance, insecurities, dissatisfaction, performance, and much more. Besides, being accountable to other fellowship members spurred them to practice the little things they were taught over and again.

Thinking about the testimonies that abounded from the fellowship groups, Luke's heart was filled with great joy.

"Even though it was really not in my plans, thanks to each and every one of you for giving me a reason to celebrate," Luke said, after he had greeted all the people present.

Standing in the middle of room, he felt led to give them a short address.

"Before we go into the festivities which I know you've all planned hard for, I'd like to tell you I'm truly grateful to have known every single one of you. With you, I've understood and experienced the God-kind of success. It's so much more than about whatever we gain or lose, for there is more to what our eyes can see . . ."

While speaking, he looked at Stephanie Lynn, who could be said to have lost everything when she decided to come clean to her followers. She and her family faced heavy criticism on social media, lost the book and TV show deals they had secured for the coming years, and had their speaking engagements cancelled. Her husband's business had not survived either, nor their daughters' popularity.

Luke then thought of Samantha, who, even though she had been forgiven by Luke, had willingly committed to repay all the money she had taken from the church treasury. His mind also went to Jide, who had ended up confessing his double-dealing to his wife Elise. The last time Luke had seen him, he was no longer wearing his wedding band.

"It's about walking on the path laid out by God for us," Luke continued. "And if we get distracted or fall outside that path, his amazing love leads us back exactly to where we are supposed to be. There is peace and abundant joy in following God's leading, no matter how painful it may seem at first or even along the way."

With a smile on his face, he once more took a look at his audience and ended his address: "So, thank you for making my journey here a successful one."

www.ingramcontent.com/pod-product-compliance
Lightning Source LLC
Chambersburg PA
CBHW071315200626
46813CB00015B/2208